Lothrop, Lee & Shepard Books   New York

The Ten-Alarm Camp-Out

BY CATHY WARREN

ILLUSTRATED BY STEVEN KELLOGG

Library of Congress Cataloging in Publication Data. Warren, Cathy. The ten-alarm camp-out. Summary: An armadillo family innocently causes havoc during their camp-out. (1. Armadillos—Fiction. 2. Counting) I. Kellogg, Steven, ill. II. Title.   PZ7.W2514Te 1983   (E)   82-24901   ISBN 0-688-02127-1   ISBN 0-688-02128-X (lib. bdg.)

For Russ, Tasha,
and Tanya Marie—C.W.

For Mother,
with gratitude for the many hours
you spent reading aloud—S.K.

Mama armadillo lives in a little house,
inside a hole, under a big oak tree.
She loves even numbers and straight lines.
She has nine babies.
"Nine plus me makes ten," she says,
"and ten is a nice even number."

She loves to take her babies on picnics and overnight camp-outs.

OUR JULY SCHEDULE
PICNICS ○ CAMP-OUTS ○

One day she lined up her babies in a nice straight row.
She gave each baby a special marching alarm clock.
Then they marched
ONE, TWO, THREE, FOUR, FIVE, SIX, SEVEN, EIGHT, NINE, TEN,
to the ticking sound of the clocks.

They camped at the top of the green hill, beneath fig trees and beside a clear stream.

They played tag.
They swam in the cool stream water.

Just as the sun was going down, Mama set each alarm
for ten o'clock.
"Ten is a nice even number," she said.
Then she lined up her babies in a nice straight row.
They curled up into little balls
and went to sleep.

Mama snored.
She snored so hard, she started to roll.
She rolled into the baby next to her,
who bumped into the baby next to him.
Soon all ten were rolling down the hill.

One rolled onto a football field.
Two rolled into a park.

Three rolled in front of a grocery store.
Four rolled into a bakery shop.

Just as the sun was coming up, the baker noticed
the four balls on the bottom shelf.
"I wonder if these round loaves are any good,"
he thought.
He took a bite.

"Aaugh! Help! What is it?" he cried.
And off he ran.

He ran past the grocery store just as the grocer was noticing the three balls next to the bananas.

"I wonder if these melons are ripe," he thought.

He took a sniff.

"Pew!" said the grocer. "These smell rotten!"

But when he picked one up and started to toss it into the trash, he heard a ticking sound.
"Help!" he cried. "It sounds like a bomb!"
And off he ran.

He ran so fast, he forgot to watch where he was going.
He tripped over two balls and bumped into the baker,
who landed in Puddle Park Pond.

"Sorry," said the grocer, "I tripped over these duck eggs."
But when he leaned down to see if they were broken,
he cried,
"Help! Dinosaurs!"

"Bombs!" cried the baker.
And off they ran.

They ran onto the football field, where the coach was
busy preparing for the game.
He saw one ball on the field.
"I wonder if that's my new ball," he thought.
He picked it up.
"Ugh," said the coach, "this ball is old and feels funny."

He tossed it over his shoulder and into the arms of the
grocer, who heard the ticking sound.
"Not me!" cried the grocer.
He tossed it to the baker,
who tossed it to the coach,
who dropped it on the field.
And off they ran.

Soon they came to the police station.
"Help!" they cried. "There are things all over the place."
"Don't worry," said the Captain,
"I'll put them in a special hole on the other side of the
green hill.
They will be safe there."

The Captain found
one on the football field,

two in the park,

three in front of the grocery store,

and four in the bakery shop.
She put them in the back of her truck.

And off she drove.
She drove so fast, the balls began to bounce.
They bounced out of the truck and
onto the top of the green hill.

The alarms went off.
The armadillos unrolled themselves.

They ate fresh figs and drank cool stream water.
"What a wonderful picnic," said some of the babies.

"What a great camp-out," said others.
"We will come again soon," promised Mama.

She lined up her babies in a nice straight row.
Then they marched
ONE, TWO, THREE, FOUR, FIVE, SIX, SEVEN, EIGHT,
NINE, TEN, to the ticking sound of the clocks.

They marched down the hill
and back to their little house,
inside a hole,
under a big oak tree.